DUPERBALL

Kes Gray

Illustrated by

Chris Mould

OX

OXFORD

UNIVERSITY PRESS

Great Clarendon Street, Oxford, OX2 6DP,
United Kingdom

Oxford University Press is a department of the University of Oxford.
It furthers the University's objective of excellence in research, scholarship,
and education by publishing worldwide. Oxford is a registered trade mark of
Oxford University Press in the UK and in certain other countries

Text © Kes Gray 2003

The moral rights of the author have been asserted

First published in this edition 2016

British Library Cataloguing in Publication Data
Data available

978-0-19-837748-1

3 5 7 9 10 8 6 4 2

Paper used in the production of this book is a natural, recyclable product
made from wood grown in sustainable forests. The manufacturing process
conforms to the environmental regulations of the country of origin.

Printed in China by Leo Paper Products Ltd.

Acknowledgements
Cover and inside illustrations by Chris Mould
Inside cover notes written by Becca Heddle

Contents

Chapter 1

The Toyshop

A long beard that sparkled like silver candyfloss. Tiny, star-shaped spectacles. A long, shimmery dress. And silver trainers with gold laces.

This was, without a doubt, the oddest-looking toyshop owner that Charlie had ever seen.

"Can I help you?" said the toyshop owner, softly.

Charlie decided he was one of three things – a wizard, an ancient rock star, or a Kung Fu master. Probably, he was all three.

"I've come to spend my pocket money," said Charlie.

"Please feel free to have a look around," smiled the Kung Fu Rock Star Wizard.

Charlie put his hand in his pocket.

"I've already had a look around. What have you got for one coin?"

The toyshop owner blinked and stroked his beard.

"One coin? Deary me. One coin? Let me see. One coin? Come with me."

Charlie went to follow the toyshop owner – but he had vanished!

"This is your lucky day!" said the shop owner, tapping Charlie on the shoulder.

Charlie spun round to find the toyshop owner standing right behind him. How he got there was anybody's guess.

"He must be a wizard," thought Charlie. "Or a time and space traveller."

The wizard-time-and-space-traveller held out his hand.

"Do you know what this is?" he said.

Charlie stared long and hard
at the object nestling in the shop
owner's hand.

"It's a super ball," said Charlie.
"Super balls are the bounciest balls you
can get."

"Close your eyes and look again," said
the toyshop owner.

"He's *definitely* a wizard," thought
Charlie. "How can I look with my
eyes closed?"

"Can you see?" said the toyshop wizard.

Charlie shook his head. "My eyes are
closed," he said.

"Shut your eyes tighter," said the Kung
Fu-Wizard-Totally-Strange-Person.
Charlie scrunched up his face.

"Now open your eyes," smiled the
toyshop owner.

Chapter 2

"Yours for One Coin!"

Charlie opened his eyes and gasped.
The super ball was glowing different
colours.

"This isn't a super ball, Charlie," said
the toyshop owner. "It's a Duperball.
It's the only Duperball in the world.
It will bounce higher than your imagination
and it is yours for just one coin."

Charlie gulped. "Wow – it must be worth more than one coin," he whispered.

"When one coin is all you have, one coin is all the money in the world," smiled the toyshop owner.

Charlie held out his hand.

The wizard took the coin and pressed the Duperball into Charlie's hand.

"Bounce the Duperball as high as you wish, Charlie. It will always come back. Have fun, but be warned. If you fail to catch it and the Duperball hits the ground it will never ever bounce for you or anyone again."

"I won't. I mean, I will," said Charlie. He closed his fingers tightly around the Duperball and ran to the toyshop door.

"Allow me," said the toyshop owner.

Charlie skidded to a stop. The toyshop owner was already holding the door of the toyshop open!

"Safe hands, Charlie. Safe hands."
He smiled.

But Charlie wasn't listening. His thoughts were bouncing higher and higher. His thoughts were with the Duperball.

Chapter 3

"I Hardly Even Bounced It!"

Charlie knew the perfect place to bounce the Duperball. The cycle path. It was perfectly smooth, with no bumps or cracks.

He ran all the way there and placed the Duperball carefully between his finger and thumb. He counted to five and let go.

The Duperball hit the ground – and shot
ten metres into the air!

Charlie cupped his hands in a mad
panic. The Duperball dropped into them
and he slammed his fingers shut.

"Wow!" thought Charlie. "I hardly
even bounced it!"

He popped the Duperball in his pocket.
It was time for tea.

When he got home he found his mum upside down, trying to get the washing machine to work. She greeted Charlie with a wave of a rubber glove.

"You've got a hole in your glove," said Charlie.

His mum poked her finger through the hole and smiled.

"I need a new pair!" she laughed.

Charlie smiled. They needed a new everything in his house.

He ran upstairs to his bedroom.

He wanted a closer look at his
Duperball.

He sat on his bed and raised it to
his eyes.

It was glowing green. No, it wasn't,
it was glowing red. No, it wasn't, it
was ... whatever it was, it was pretty cool.

Teatime came and went in its usual

crispy-crumb way. Dad came home from
work and was immediately handed the
rubber gloves.

"There are holes in *two* fingers, now,"
he said, squeezing them on.

Charlie headed for the door.
It was time for another bounce!

Chapter 4

"Higher than Your Imagination"

This time Charlie made his way to school. He knew the big playground there would be empty after lessons on a Friday.

Charlie had always been good at catching. He was goalie for the school football team and wicket keeper in cricket. You could say that Charlie Benson had some of the safest hands in town.

It wasn't long before he was sending the Duperball twenty, thirty, forty, fifty metres into the sky and catching it every time.

With every expert flick of his wrist the Duperball pinged off the playground surface and rocketed higher and higher into the sky.

"One more bounce before bedtime," Charlie decided. "This time it's the Big One!"

He paused and took a deep, excited breath. He rubbed the Duperball on his jumper for luck. He gave it a kiss for double luck.

He counted to ten and then hurled the Duperball at the ground.

It bounced off the ground like an elastic kangaroo with a rocket up its bottom.

Charlie gulped. He couldn't see it anywhere. The Duperball had gone higher than he had ever imagined.

It was just like the toyshop owner had said.

Charlie waited. He waited and waited and waited. He scraped the toes of his shoes on the ground. He tied his shoelaces and hopped up and down.

It was getting late. The sun had almost disappeared behind the school building and still there was no sign of the Duperball.

Charlie was about to give up and walk home when his fingers began to tingle. He peered up into the sky. There was definitely something up there.

His fingers tingletingled. They could feel the Duperball arriving. Charlie's heart leaped. He could *see* the Duperball arriving!

The light was fading fast, but the colours of the Duperball helped to guide his hands. He could see it clearly now. It was glowing silver like a meteor and racing towards him.

Charlie raised his arms and then ...

CLAP!

His hands shut fast around it.

"Am I pleased to see you!" said Charlie, slipping the Duperball back into his trouser pocket.

Back home, he found Dad fiddling with the leaky tap. "Three fingers gone on these gloves!" he shouted as Charlie raced into the kitchen. "And one of the thumbs is on its way out, too!"

"Why don't you buy a new pair?"
Charlie asked his mum.

"New things cost money, Charlie," said
his mum.

Charlie shrugged and went upstairs to
bed. He was worn out.

He put the Duperball in his pyjamas
and patted his pocket.

"Sunday tomorrow," he smiled, "and
the sky's the limit!"

Chapter 5

Is It a Planet?
Is It a Star?

Next morning, Charlie dressed quickly and sprinted into the kitchen for his breakfast.

"Come and look at this!" shouted his dad from the living room.

Charlie carried his breakfast bowl into the living room and joined his mum and dad on the sofa.

"Maybe there *is* life on Mars!" chuckled his dad.

Charlie looked at the TV screen. Lots of space experts were sitting round a table looking very serious and passing around photos.

One man was droning on about satellites. Another woman was showing pictures of planets.

Then there was this clip of an old black and white space film with monsters that weren't in the slightest bit scary.

Now it was more pictures of more stars, and ... then ...

Charlie stared hard at the screen.

His Duperball was on TV!

In space!

It had been photographed by space cameras in actual space!

Charlie listened. None of the scientists knew what it was.

They couldn't even *guess* what it was!

Charlie slipped his hand inside his pocket and a rush of excitement surged through his fingers.

"Bye Dad, bye Mum," he said, bouncing off the sofa and out of the house. "I'm going over to the park!"

Outside in the street, everyone was walking around glued to their Sunday papers.

Everywhere Charlie looked, there were front-page photos of his Duperball.

Charlie ran to the park and looked towards the tennis courts.

"Good," he thought. "They're empty."

In a second, he was pushing open the
gate and standing in position.

"Five, four, three, two, one,
LIFT OFF!" he cried, unleashing his arm
with downward turbo thrust.

The Duperball launched itself off
the pink surface of th tennis court and
hurtled up through the clouds and miles
into the sky.

Charlie sat on the swings for a
couple of hours and waited for his fingers
to tingle.

At long last, the tingletingle came.
He jumped down off the swing and ran
back to the tennis court.

People were playing tennis on his
launch pad!

Charlie looked up at the sky, directly above their heads. Sure enough, the Duperball was returning to earth. It was dropping at a speed of around one mile per second. He had no time to lose.

"Five, four, three, two, one, go!" he said to himself, leaping in front of the players and racing towards the net.

"Oi!" shouted the player nearest to Charlie, swinging his tennis racket wildly.

The racket hit Charlie on the
shoulder. Charlie tripped, toppled off
balance and crashed into the net.

He closed his eyes and lunged forward.
But his outstretched fingers tangled
helplessly in the net.

His eyes flashed up towards the
Duperball as it plummeted back
to Earth.

He stretched out both hands in a
desperate attempt to catch it. But he was
flat out with his legs in the air. He was
never going to reach it.

When he opened his eyes, his head was spinning. He blinked. And then he blinked again.

The Duperball was nestled behind his ear. It had landed on the net cord, rolled along the net, and dropped into the hood of Charlie's sweatshirt.

"Thank goodness!" panted Charlie. "It didn't touch the ground!"

The tennis players didn't know whether to be cross or send Charlie to hospital.

Charlie said sorry and limped off the court.

"I wonder how high it went that time?" he grinned.

Chapter 6

The Universe and Beyond

The answer was all over the early evening news. The Duperball had bounced higher than Mars, higher than Jupiter, and right up through the rings of Saturn. It had even bounced off a spaceman's helmet on the way down.

There were pictures of it everywhere and everyone was talking about it.

The Prime Minister of the United Kingdom, the President of the United States, the King of Mars, everyone in the Solar System and beyond was in a complete panic over Charlie's Duperball.

Charlie went back to the school playground again and again. Each time he bounced the Duperball as high as his imagination would let him. And even further!

On Monday it bounced as high as Uranus.

On Tuesday it bounced as high as Neptune.

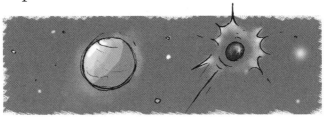

Thursday's satellite pictures snapped the Duperball whizzing out of the Solar System!

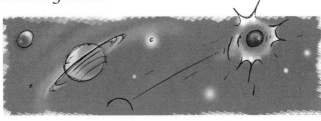

Charlie's Duperball was the biggest story in the world.

But Charlie was careful to keep it
a secret.

He didn't tell Mum, he didn't tell Dad,
and he didn't tell his friends.

He was sure everyone would want a
bounce and then one of them would drop
it. He kept the Duperball in his pyjamas at
night and in his pocket at school.

In the playground, he wrapped it in
a tissue for extra care.

When the Friday school bell rang,
Charlie sprinted home.

Tonight was the Huge One. Tonight was
the Universe and Beyond.

When he got home, his mum was upside down as usual, bashing the washing machine with a wooden spoon.

"Seven holes in seven fingers," she shouted, flapping the rubber gloves at him as he ran past.

Charlie charged straight in and out, leaving a tornado of school clothes across the bedroom floor.

He arrived at the playground in double quick time and waited until it was empty. Then he raced to his usual launching pad.

He stopped, and took some deep, deep breaths.

Even the Duperball seemed excited, glowing colours and shades that Charlie had never seen before.

Charlie gripped it extra tight and slowly began to whirl his bouncing arm round and round, like a windmill. He took the deepest breath of his life and raised the Duperball as high above his head as he could.

Then, with a lightning flick of his wrist, he blammed it against the floor.

The Duperball was gone in an instant.

It bounced somewhere between the stratosphere and the ionosphere in about five seconds, and was probably approaching Neptune as Charlie left the playground.

Chapter 7

"Gloves at the Ready"

After a week of wild newspaper excitement and frenzied news flashes, Charlie's fingers began to tingle. The Duperball was on its way home.

When Charlie arrived at school, the playground was full of cars. Charlie was too busy thinking about the Duperball to wonder why. He was just glad to see that the place where he needed to stand had been left empty.

The tingles in his fingers were growing stronger by the second.

Charlie was sure the Duperball would be back in the Earth's atmosphere inside ten minutes.

His gaze soared upwards into the sky.

Then he looked down at all the cars that were parked around him. He'd never seen cars quite like them. They had strange number plates. And the windows were so black, you couldn't see inside them.

He looked up at the clouds again and a big smile broke across his face.

"There it is," he beamed. "Come on Duperball! Come home to Charlie!"

Sure enough, three minutes earlier than Charlie's tingles had told him, the Duperball was returning to earth.

It was gleaming and glittering and spinning as it fell.

Charlie got ready. His fingers were tingletingling. He raised his arms high above his head and clasped his hands together.

The tingles had almost reached his fingernails now.

He took a deep breath. He had to concentrate. He had to focus. He stretched out his fingers.

But then he gasped, sharply. His eyes went right, his legs went left. Someone had barged him out of the way!

"Gloves at the ready!" shouted a loud, echoey voice.

Charlie looked round in dazed confusion. He had been shoved out of the way by a scientist he had seen on the telly!

"He must have been hiding in one of those cars with black windows!" thought Charlie.

The scientist had a loudspeaker in his hand and he was shouting in all directions to astronauts in silver suits.

They were throwing their space gloves on the floor and putting baseball gloves on instead.

Charlie watched helplessly as they ran to where he had been standing and held their baseball gloves up to the sky.

The Duperball was approaching fast, but it was impossible for Charlie to get close.

"Catch it!" screamed the scientist, as the Duperball fell to Earth.

Silver suits leaped and baseball gloves grabbed. The astronauts crunched into a glittering heap – and the Duperball thudded on to the floor of the playground.

It landed like a blob of wet clay and turned the same grey colour.

"WE'VE GOT IT!" cheered the scientist, scraping it up off the floor.

"YOU DROPPED IT!" moaned Charlie. "It will never bounce again."

But no one was listening.

The scientist stared Charlie straight in the eye.

"By the powers invested in me by the World Space Institute I am taking this object, for the purpose of scientific and space research. Now, clear off, kid!"

Charlie turned head over heels right through the middle of the astronauts, pulled a face and ran for home.

"You're all a bunch of butter-fingered space bores!" he yelled.

No one bothered to chase him. The scientist and the astronauts had what they had come for. Black windows closed, doors slammed, tyres screeched and the mysterious cars sped out of the playground.

Chapter 8

"What Are Those?"

When Charlie skidded into the kitchen, his mum and dad were underneath the sink again, taking it in turns with the yellow rubber gloves.

"Ten holes in ten fingers!" they said with a wave.

"One pair each!" said Charlie, excitedly.

His mum and dad crawled out backwards and wiped their brows.

"Goodness me, Charlie, what are those?" said his mum.

Charlie smiled. He was holding out two pairs of astronaut gloves.

"They're extra-strong, titanium-reinforced, never-wear-out kitchen gloves!"

Charlie's mum and dad could hardly wait to try them on.

"Ooh, Charlie," beamed Mum. "They're super!"

"No, they're not," laughed Charlie. "They're Duper!"

About the author

I remember when super balls were
first invented.

I couldn't wait to bounce mine.

I would stand on the pavement in front
of my house, while my best friend
Tim stood in my back garden ready to
catch it.

After one or two bounces my super ball
would always be lost. But that was OK.
Because the disappointment of losing it
was nothing compared to the thrill of the
bounce!